Hello, Family Members,

Learning to read is one of the most important accomplishments of early childhood. **Hello Reader!** books are designed to help children become skilled readers who like to read. Beginning readers learn to read by remembering frequently used words like "the," "is," and "and"; by using phonics skills to decode new words; and by interpreting picture and text clues. These books provide both the stories children enjoy and the structure they need to read fluently and independently. Here are suggestions for helping your child *before*, *during*, and *after* reading:

Before

- Look at the cover and pictures and have your child predict what the story is about.
- Read the story to your child.
- Encourage your child to chime in with familiar words and phrases.
- Echo read with your child by reading a line first and having your child read it after you do.

During

- Have your child think about a word he or she does not recognize right away. Provide hints such as "Let's see if we know the sounds" and "Have we read other words like this one?"
- Encourage your child to use phonics skills to sound out new words.
- Provide the word for your child when more assistance is needed so that he or she does not struggle and the experience of reading with you is a positive one.
- Encourage your child to have fun by reading with a lot of expression . . . like an actor!

After

- Have your child keep lists of interesting and favorite words.
- Encourage your child to read the books over and over again. Have him or her read to brothers, sisters, grandparents, and even teddy bears. Repeated readings develop confidence in young readers.
- Talk about the stories. Ask and answer questions. Share ideas about the funniest and most interesting characters and events in the stories.

I do hope that you and your child enjoy this book.

—Francie Alexander
Chief Education Officer,
Scholastic's Learning Ventures

To Jean and Phoebe
—B.C. & G.M.

To Adam, Laura, and Leslie
—G.B.K.

Originally published under the title *School Friends #4: Brenda's Private Swing* by Scholastic Inc.
Text copyright © 1990 by Grace Maccarone and Bernice Chardiet.
Illustrations copyright © 1990 by Chardiet Unlimited, Inc.

All rights reserved. Published by Scholastic Inc. Produced by Chardiet Unlimited, Inc. SCHOLASTIC, HELLO READER, CARTWHEEL BOOKS and associated logos are trademarks and/or registered trademarks of Scholastic Inc.

Library of Congress Cataloging-in-Publication Data available.

ISBN 0-439-35853-1

12 11 10 9 8 7 6   06

Printed in the U.S.A.
This edition first printing, April 2002

SCHOOL FRIENDS

The Playground Bully

Originally titled: *Brenda's Private Swing*

by Bernice Chardiet and Grace Maccarone
Illustrated by G. Brian Karas

Hello Reader! — Level 3

SCHOLASTIC INC. Cartwheel ·B·O·O·K·S·®

New York   Toronto   London   Auckland   Sydney
Mexico City   New Delhi   Hong Kong   Buenos Aires

A cool breeze tickled Bunny's face.
It tickled her eyes, her nose, and her lips.
Bunny laughed as she pumped back
and forth on Brenda's new swing set.

Bunny wished she could swing all day.

"You have to stop now!" Brenda said.
"That's mean," said Bunny.
"This is my private playground," Brenda said.
"And I'm the boss."

"May I go on the slide?"
Bunny asked.
Brenda thought for a minute.
"All right," she said.

Bunny went up the ladder
and down the slide.
Her sneakers stuck as she slid.
It was not a good ride.

Bunny didn't want to slide again.

Bunny sat on the lawn.
She looked at Brenda.
She looked at the empty swing.
Just then, Martin walked by.

"Can I go on your swing?" he asked Brenda.
"All right," Brenda said.
Martin ran to the swing.
He had a big smile on his face.

Martin started to swing back and forth.
"You have to stop now," said Brenda.
"But I just started," said Martin.
"This is my private playground," Brenda said.
"And I want Bunny to use it now."

Martin got off the swing.
He went down the slide.
Then he walked up the slide.
"Don't go up the slide that way,"
Brenda said. "You have to follow my rules."

Martin sat on top of the slide
and watched the girls swing.
Then he remembered what he had
in his pocket—a box of Fruity Chewies.
Martin popped a cherry chewie in
his mouth.

Brenda was watching.
"Give me the rest and you can go
on the swing," she said.
Martin quickly slid down.
He gave Brenda the box of chewies.
Bunny had to get off the swing.
She watched Martin swing
until it was time to go home.

Two days later, Bunny was back at
Brenda's house.
Bunny was having a good, long swing.
Then Martin came.
"May I swing?" he asked.
"Maybe," said Brenda.
Martin took out a box of Gummy Bears.
"You can have these," he said.
"Okay," said Brenda.

This time Bunny was ready.
"I'll give you a chocolate bar," she said.
Brenda took the Gummy Bears.
Then she took the chocolate bar.
"The two of you have to share the swing,"
she said. "It's Martin's turn, now."

Bunny got off the swing.
Martin got on the swing.
Martin swung for a short time.
"Now it's Bunny's turn," Brenda said.

Martin got off the swing.
Bunny got on the swing.
Bunny swung for a short time.
"Now it's Martin's turn," Brenda said.

Then it was Bunny's turn again.
And then it was Martin's turn again.
"This isn't much fun at all,"
Bunny thought.

Sammy came and saw them.
He asked to go on the swing.
"Only if you give me candy,"
Brenda said. "That's the rule."

Sammy ran home.

He came back with a bag of jelly beans.

He gave the jelly beans to Brenda.

"May I swing now?" he asked.

"No," said Brenda.

"I hate jelly beans."

Sammy ran home again.
He came back with a Tootsie Roll.
Brenda let him swing.

Now, everyone who went on Brenda's
swing had to give her candy.
But one day, Bunny had no candy.

She looked all over the kitchen for
something else.
Then she saw some fancy pastries.
Her mother was saving them for company.
But Bunny needed something for Brenda.

She took one pastry.
It had layers of cream and a flaky crust.
The top had white frosting with chocolate
squiggles.
It was Bunny's favorite.

Brenda liked the pastry very much.
Bunny was swinging back and forth
when Martin came by.

"What do you have for me?" Brenda asked.
"My mother wouldn't let me have any candy
today," Martin said.
"Too bad," said Brenda. "Then you
can't swing."
"*Please*," said Martin. "I'll give you something
tomorrow. *Please!*"
"No," said Brenda.

Bunny was having a long swing.
But this time it wasn't fun.
She felt bad because Martin looked so sad.
And she felt bad because she had taken
the pastry.

That night, Bunny told her mother,
"I took a pastry."
"That's all right," her mother said.
"I bought an extra one just for you.
But next time, you should tell me first."

The next day Bunny and Martin were
having lunch at school.
"What do you have for Brenda today?"
Bunny asked.
Martin looked in his lunch box.
"A box of Fruity Chewies," he said.

"I have two chocolate marshmallow
cookies," said Bunny.
"But I wish I could keep them for myself."
"Me, too," said Martin.

Just then, Brenda came by.
"Oooh! My favorites," she said.

Brenda grabbed the Fruity Chewies.
"No," said Martin.
Brenda reached for a cookie.
"No," said Bunny.
"You'll be sorry when you want to use my private playground," Brenda said.

"No, we won't!" Bunny shouted.

Brenda stuck out her tongue and
walked away.

"Let's play checkers after school,"
Martin said.
"Okay," said Bunny. "Would you like a
chocolate marshmallow cookie, Martin?'"
"Yes," said Martin. "Here, have a
Fruity Chewie. Bossy Brenda can play
by herself today."